OUROBOROS

Tre Chado

Ouroboros: Bloodline of the Tide Book 3, Years after Helen's bloodline tried to outrun the western shore, Rayne grows up in Rayden's Ridge, a village built on silence, distance, and forgotten truth.

But when Rayne discovers Grace Fana's hidden journal, the old covenant begins to wake. Drawn west by dreams, ancestral memory, and the pull of buried names, Rayne leaves with her cousins, Chase and Callie, only to find that the land has never forgotten what the people tried to hide.

As salt rises, bones speak, and the Ridge begins to crack, one generation must face what the others buried. The covenant cannot be carried by one sacrifice anymore. It must be remembered by all.

Ouroboros is the final turn in the bloodline's story—a tale of memory, sacrifice, silence, and the circle that keeps deciding what must live, what must die, and what must return.

COPYRIGHT

ISBN: 978-1-968581-07-7 {Papeback}

ISBN: 978-1-968581-06-0 {Online}

This is a work of fiction. Names, characters, places, and incidents are either the product of the author's imagination or used fictitiously. Any resemblance to actual events, locales, or persons, living or dead, is purely coincidental.

Printed in the United States of America

DEDICATION

For those who carry memory in blood and in spirit.

CHAPTER LIST

CHAPTER 1: THE NEW GENERATION

The wind in the inland hills never spoke.

It moved like silence, brushing gently through stalks of cane and corn, gliding across thatched zinc rooftops, pressing against the skin of children who had never known danger—only warning. This was not the sea wind of the western shore, where the stories lived. It was mostly dry and hushed, like a lullaby whispered by a land that hadn't buried much.

Rayne was born into that hush.

Her mother, Laura, was a woman of order. She woke with the sun, and her prayers smelled like warm cassava and neem leaves. Her father, Alwin, worked the soil like it was gospel—hands dark and blistered, stained with ancestral offerings he didn't speak of anymore. There was no shrine in their home, only a closed room with limited capacity, where the corners smelled like white sage and the old window never opened.

The elders called the place Rayden's Ridge. They said it was safe because it was far from the western coast—far from the bloodline that had once called "trouble into the bone." Most of the children here never knew the stories. Not really. Just shadows—the kind you hear half-sleep or in the creak of trees. But Rayne had always known she was being watched when she stared into the abyss of the forest.

At night, her dreams bled.

She would wake with the taste of ash in her mouth, sweat soaking her temples, echoes of chanting in a language she didn't understand. A woman with dark skin like burnt cedar and eyes glowing white would appear in the dreamscape—sometimes standing in water, sometimes at the edge of fire—always whispering:

"Return."

But return where?

Rayne had never left.

ΔΔΔ

It was during the Season of Smoke and Rain that things changed. Shadows moved when the humid winds came early, and the sky turned overcast before the fall of dusk. That's when Rayne found the journal.

It was wrapped in oil cloth and hidden beneath an old floorboard in her father's locked room—a room she had never been allowed to enter. Alwin had forgotten to lock it one day, and something pulled her in. Not voluntarily. The pressure voluntold her.

Beneath the oil cloth, the journal was thick, bound in dried banana leaves, the ink faded but legible. She opened to the first page. The handwriting was strong but feminine, and the name written on the inside cover stopped her breath cold:

Grace Fana.

A name not spoken in Rayden's Ridge.

The next pages told stories she had never been told—a mother named Helen, a cursed bloodline, a village by the sea, a woman who tried to bind spirits and ended up unleashing something older than the legends themselves.

The deeper she read, the more her bones ached. Her dreams sharpened. The chanting grew louder. The woman in her visions now had a name: Grace. And her words became clearer:

"The west remembers."

ΔΔΔ

About an hour before dinner, Rayne tried to show her parents the journal. Alwin struck it from her hands before she could finish explaining. It hit the floor hard, pages spreading like something wounded. Laura stared at the name Grace Fana as if it had opened a door she had spent her whole life pretending was only a wall.

"Where did you find this?" Alwin asked, but his voice already knew.

Rayne tried to answer, but Laura had begun to cry—not loud, not broken, just silently, the way people cry when the subconscious pokes a hole through the lie they were forced to live inside. Alwin picked up the journal and carried it back to the locked room. Then he shut the door, nailed it closed, and said nothing else.

ΔΔΔ

The dreams didn't just come to Rayne anymore. That evening, while the family gathered for dinner, Christian said he had seen a girl made of wind standing outside his goat pen. No one laughed. No one asked him twice. The family elders grew afraid, but fear did not stop the night from moving.

Later, when Chase and Callie were sent down to the riverbed for water, Rayne followed. That was when she heard them speaking in Merican—the forgotten freedom language—softly at first, then clearer, like the words had been waiting in their mouths. And when they reached the river, it was gone. Not low. Not shallow. Gone. The stones were wet. The mud was fresh. But the water had dried in one night.

They ran back to tell the adults. Lanterns were lit. Voices rose. Christian, Alwin, Laura, and the others hurried down to the riverbed, but by the time they arrived, the water had returned—flowing calm and steady, as if it had never left. The adults stood there in silence, staring at the river with doubt already creeping into their faces. Then a gust moved through the trees, low and sudden, brushing past the children but leaving the adults untouched. Rayne heard it. Chase heard it. Callie heard it too.

"Return."

ΔΔΔ

She told Chase and Callie to meet her under the bone fig tree, just past the old yam fields. When Rayne packed the satchel, the journal was already inside. She knew she had not placed it there. She knew Alwin had locked it away. Still, there it was—wrapped again, waiting like it had never intended to stay behind.

They walked at dusk, when the land was softest—when the silence was most willing to open. They took no machetes. No maps. Told no adults. Only the journal, the wind, and the hum in their blood knew their destination.

The journey west was not long by distance, but each step felt like walking into older skin, into stories pressed deep into the earth. Trees grew denser. Birds vanished. Even the insects grew quiet. At one point, Chase stopped and whispered:

"Do you hear that?"

Rayne nodded. There was music somewhere ahead. Faint. Off-key.

Familiar.

At the first marker—a pile of stones shaped like a ribcage—Callie knelt to touch the earth, then pulled her hand back as if stung.

"It's warm."

The air began to shift. And that's when they saw her.

A woman in white, walking through the mist as if she were made of it. Her feet were nowhere in sight. Her eyes were the same glowing white as in Rayne's dreams. She did not speak with her mouth.

"You walk where oaths were broken."

Callie screamed. Chase tried to run but tripped over roots that now held him fast. Rayne stood still. Something in her recognized the woman.

"Grace," she said aloud.

The woman blinked. The fog swallowed her.

ΔΔΔ

Meanwhile, in Rayden's Ridge, Laura would later remember the feeling more than the reason. The tightness in her chest. The heat in her throat. The book hitting the floor. Rayne's name sitting on her tongue like a warning she could no longer understand. She could not remember why she had been angry—only that she had been.

So she moved through the day under the usual pretense—boiling water, folding cloth, sweeping dust from corners already clean—while something soft and unseen settled over the village. It pressed against thought and memory alike, dulling the edges of concern, making the children's absence feel distant, almost ordinary, like something that could wait.

Rayne's name slipped first. Not gone. Just harder to reach. Then Chase's. Then Callie's. The worry remained, but it had no shape to hold on to. It became easier to believe they had been sent somewhere safe. Somewhere known. Somewhere the adults had already agreed upon, even if none of them could remember agreeing.

ΔΔΔ

Farther west, the children were still walking. What was meant to be a short walk had already folded into night. Rayne, Chase, and Callie moved beneath a sky that seemed to forget the sun, their steps guided by something deeper than thought—something that did not ask, only led. By the time anyone in Rayden's Ridge might have thought to look, they had already reached the home of a forgotten village—what remained of Helen's last stand and Grace's echoes. Roofs caved in. Walls cracked. But in the center, untouched, stood a stone altar covered in moss and dried flowers that refused to wilt.

The air smelled like salt and iron.

Rayne stepped forward, the journal in her hand. She opened to the final page. A prayer was written there—part chant, part song, part warning. Full of danger.

She didn't know why, but she read it aloud.

The wind stopped.

The earth hummed.

And beneath their feet, the altar glowed faintly—red, then white, then black.

The covenant stirred.

And the land began to remember.

ΔΔΔ

They slept in what had once been a schoolhouse, bones of chalk still dusting the floor. That night, the dreams came not in fragments, but in full.

Rayne found herself back at the altar, but this time it was complete and shining. She was surrounded by hundreds of women and men in deep blue robes, their faces veiled. In front of them stood a figure she had only ever seen drawn in charcoal sketches:

Grace.

The woman raised her arms.

“Today, we bind spirit to land, and blood to silence. Not for power, but for peace.”

But behind her, in the crowd, someone whispered:

“She lies.”

Then came fire.

The dream shattered with a scream.

Rayne woke to see Callie curled in the corner, whispering, “She’s in my skin... she’s in my skin.” Chase stood over her, shaking, his hands bleeding. The journal lay open, its pages now unreadable—not burned, but soaked with saltwater.

“Rayne,” he said, “we should not be here.”

Rayne stared at the altar glowing in the distance.

“No,” she whispered. “We have to be.”

CHAPTER 2: NAMES IN THE ASH

Morning came without light. The sun rose late over the ruins, its rays weak—veiled behind a gray sky heavy with stillness. The kind of stillness that listens. That watches. That waits.

Rayne sat on the broken steps of the schoolhouse, the journal clutched in her lap though the words were now gone, erased by saltwater that came from nowhere. She hadn't slept again. Every time her eyes closed, she saw fire wrapped in song, and Grace's face—proud and afraid at once.

Behind her, Callie lay under a wool shawl, eyes half-open, trembling as if sleep had taken her body but left something else awake inside her. Chase paced like a trapped dog, eyes red from fear or fury—Rayne couldn't tell which.

"We go back today," he said, not looking at her. "We ain't supposed to be here. Something's wrong with Callie. You saw it."

Rayne didn't answer. Her fingers kept brushing over the last page of the journal—a page that no longer existed but still pulsed in her mind.

"The altar… it moved," she whispered.

Chase stopped pacing. “What?”

“It wasn’t just glowing. It moved. Shifted. I heard it breathing.”

He stepped forward, voice low. “Rayne, you need to stop talking like that.”

But the wind rose again—soft at first, then layered with that familiar hum. Not a song. Not a language. A memory.

Rayne stood. “We keep going... or go back on your own.”

Chase grabbed her arm. “No. We go back. We get the elders.”

She turned slowly. “The elders are the reason no one talks about this. You want to bring this back to Rayden’s Ridge and wake up to salt in your mouth every morning?”

Chase didn’t let go.

“Callie’s not well. She’s burning up.”

“Then she needs to reach the next place. Whatever’s inside her wants to finish something. It’s not sickness, it’s calling.”

“She’s twelve, Rayne.”

“And I’m fifteen,” Rayne snapped. “Old enough to know I’m not imagining what I saw.”

A groan came from behind them. Callie sat up slowly, her eyes half-lidded, her voice not quite her own.

"The path is waiting."

Chase stepped back. Rayne froze.

"Callie?" she said.

Callie blinked. "The altar marked us. The land opened. We can't stop, not now."

She stood barefoot and pointed into the jungle. "There."

No one argued after that.

ΔΔΔ

They followed Callie. Barefoot, silent, unwavering—she moved like she had walked this path before. As if the mud knew her name, and the trees leaned away to let her pass.

The deeper they went, the less the world looked like the one they'd known. The vines grew longer, the trees taller, the ground too soft, too warm. Leaves turned black at the edges. Chase flinched every time a branch brushed his shoulder. Rayne kept the journal against her chest, even though its pages were turning blank.

"What is this place?" Chase whispered.

Rayne didn't answer. She was listening—not to him, but to the rhythm beneath her feet. There was a pulse in the ground. Slow. Measured. Like a heartbeat. It matched the one in her chest.

Callie stopped suddenly, at the edge of a wide clearing.

In the center stood a tree like none they'd ever seen—massive, twisted, its bark as pale as bone, and around it, dozens of totems carved from stone and wood. Some had faces. Some had mouths. All were turned inward, toward the tree.

"They call it the Witness Tree," Callie said.

Rayne's skin prickled.

Chase stepped forward. "Callie, how do you know that?"

Callie smiled, and for a moment, it wasn't her smile.

Rayne pulled her cousin back gently. "Let me go first."

She stepped into the clearing. As soon as her foot touched the grass, all sound stopped. The wind, the birds, even Chase's breath. Silence thick as oil.

The tree's bark shifted. A pattern formed in it—a spiral with an open eye. Rayne blinked.

The eye blinked back.

She stepped back nervously.

ΔΔΔ

The clearing began to thin around her. The trees stretched tall, then blurred at the edges. The Witness Tree blinked once more, and the ground beneath Rayne's feet turned slick, reflecting a sky that was no longer there. When she opened her eyes again, she was no longer in the clearing.

She stood in a hall of mirrors—not glass, but still water, flat and unmoving. Each reflection showed a different version of her: one smiling, one burning, one with black eyes and salt pouring from her mouth.

A voice echoed.

"You carry her blood."

Rayne turned, but saw no one.

"You woke the altar. Now you must carry the path."

“Who are you?” she called.

"I am what your people left behind."

Suddenly, one of the mirrors cracked—then another—then another—until they all shattered at once, and she was falling.

Falling into a scream.

ΔΔΔ

She woke on the ground, mouth full of dirt, tears streaming.

Callie stood over her. “It showed you something, didn’t it?”

Rayne nodded, too breathless to speak.

“We’re being tested,” Callie said softly. “We each have to face something of our own.”

Chase looked panicked. “No. No. No. We need to leave. This is wrong. This... this is evil.”

“No,” Rayne rasped. “It’s ancient.”

Then the wind picked up again—this time strong, loud, moaning like a mother in mourning.

From behind the Witness Tree, something began to rise. A figure cloaked in smoke and feathers. Its face was hidden, but its voice was clear.

"You trespass on sacred bindings."

Chase pulled Rayne back. "We're sorry. We didn't mean to..."

"Lies," the spirit hissed. "The land called. You answered. Now you must finish what the blood began."

The spirit raised its hand. The ground cracked.

From the earth came whispers. From the trees, eyes. The totems began to hum.

"Go," the spirit said. "Follow the roots. Reach the mouth of salt. Or be swallowed like the rest."

Then it vanished.

Rayne, still on the ground, looked at the cracked soil beneath her.

Thin red threads ran through it.

Veins.

Leading west.

She stood.

"Come on," she whispered. "This is the path."

ΔΔΔ

They walked until dusk. No one spoke.

Callie's silence had grown eerie—too controlled. Chase muttered prayers under his breath. The trees had begun to change again. Their leaves shimmered like fish scales. The sky pulsed in slow waves of gold and ash.

Finally, they reached another marker: a circle of stones shaped like teeth, with a single flat slab in the center.

A message was carved into it:

"One must stay. One must forget. One must bleed."

Rayne read it aloud.

Chase stepped back. "What does that mean?"

Callie looked at Rayne, eyes cold. "It means we're not all meant to finish this journey."

Rayne swallowed hard.

She looked at the stone again. Then at the land. Then at her cousins.

And realized: the path wasn't just testing them.

It was choosing.

CHAPTER 3: THE EDGE OF THE WEST

Rayne didn't sleep that night. She lay curled beside the stone slab, eyes wide, staring at the canopy above as it shifted slowly, impossibly—like the trees themselves were breathing. The message on the stone echoed in her chest: "One must stay. One must forget. One must bleed."

The land had spoken.

The path had chosen.

But it hadn't said who.

Callie muttered in her sleep again, sweat beading at her temples. She spoke in a language Rayne and Chase could barely recognize. It sounded like Merican with a Cajun dialect. It was hard to tell.

Chase stayed awake too, hands clutching a carved branch like a weapon.

In the deep part of the night, Rayne felt the shift.

The ground pulsed once—like a drumbeat.

And the altar in her mind opened.

ΔΔΔ

She was dreaming again—or maybe she wasn't.

The world looked like water, but it held her like stone. She stood inside a ruined temple. The walls were made of coral and bone. At the far end, a single figure waited, seated on a black throne.

Her skin shimmered gold, and her eyes burned white.

Grace.

But not as Rayne had seen her in sketches or on the journey to the west. This Grace was alive with power, draped in sea-colored robes and crowned with ash. Her voice came not from her mouth, but from the walls themselves.

"You crossed the line they buried. You've awakened what we once sealed."

Rayne stepped closer. "Tell me what to do."

"The covenant sleeps beneath the altar. It dreams in salt and root. But blood remembers. And now it stirs."

"I don't understand..."

"You don't have to. You just have to choose."

Rayne's breath caught. "Choose what?"

But Grace was gone.

The coral crumbled.

The water screamed.

ΔΔΔ

Rayne awoke to Callie sitting upright, eyes wide open and unblinking.

"The covenant is calling," Callie said.

Chase scrambled to his feet. "I'm not going any farther. I'll wait here. You go. Whatever this is—it's got nothing to do with me."

Callie turned her head slowly toward him. "It has everything to do with you."

Rayne stood, wiping dust from her face. "You saw something too, didn't you?"

Chase didn't answer.

They packed in silence and followed the red threads through the jungle. The path became thinner, less like earth and more like bone. Trees hung low, whispering. At one point, they passed a field of dolls—hundreds of them, strung from branches by their necks with red ribbons. Their eyes had been replaced with shells.

Chase whispered, "What is this place?"

Callie answered, "Where the covenant was written."

ΔΔΔ

By midday, the threads led them to a wide basin of salt—cracked, glowing, endless. At the center rose a broken altar, half-buried in brine and shadow.

Rayne stepped forward first.

The salt stung her eyes and her lungs, but she didn't stop. The closer she got, the more the air trembled. The altar had once been carved with glyphs, now eaten by time. The ground beneath it pulsed red—the same pulse she'd felt in the clearing.

She dropped to her knees.

Laid a hand on the stone.

It opened.

Not like a door, but like skin parting by a knife.

A deep breath exhaled from below—hot, bitter, sacred.

Callie gasped and dropped to her knees. Chase fell backward. From the earth rose voices—dozens, maybe hundreds—speaking over each other in chants and cries and lullabies.

Rayne heard her name.

And Grace's.

And a familiar yet distant name…

Helen's.

"We bound it here… We sealed it with song… We buried it in daughters…"

The altar glowed again—red, then white, then black. A symbol burned into Rayne's palm.

She screamed.

Chase grabbed her, tried to pull her back, but the altar wasn't finished.

It reached.

A tendril of smoke wrapped around Callie's throat. Rayne leapt forward and slapped her cousin's back—and the smoke released

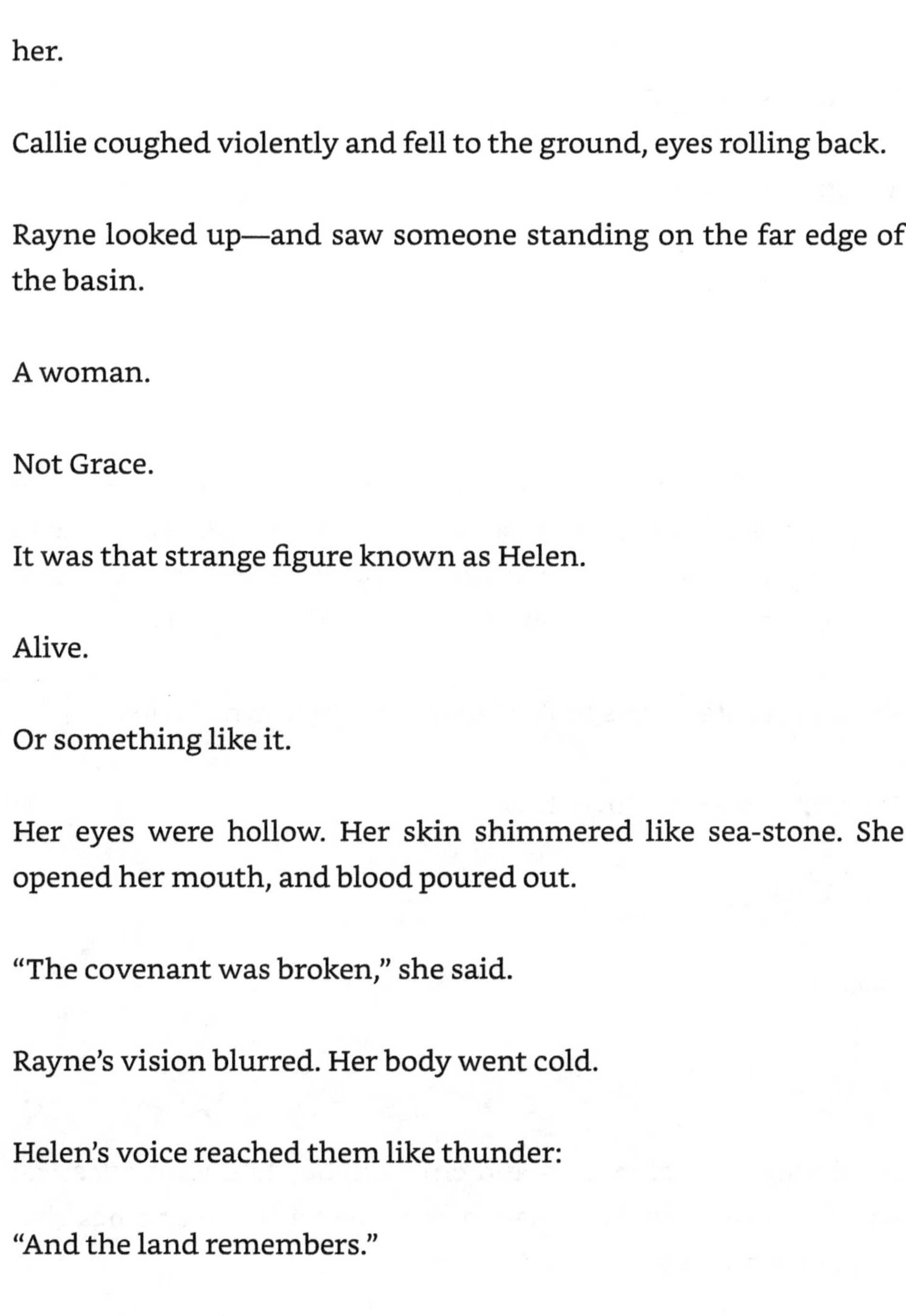

her.

Callie coughed violently and fell to the ground, eyes rolling back.

Rayne looked up—and saw someone standing on the far edge of the basin.

A woman.

Not Grace.

It was that strange figure known as Helen.

Alive.

Or something like it.

Her eyes were hollow. Her skin shimmered like sea-stone. She opened her mouth, and blood poured out.

“The covenant was broken,” she said.

Rayne’s vision blurred. Her body went cold.

Helen’s voice reached them like thunder:

“And the land remembers.”

Then she vanished.

The altar shattered.

The ground cracked.

And the salt began to sink.

ΔΔΔ

Rayne stumbled backward, dragging Callie with her, her feet slipping on the brittle white crust as it cracked like eggshells beneath them. Chase screamed something—a warning or a prayer—but it was drowned out by the sound of the earth tearing open.

From the center of the broken altar, a chasm yawned wide.

It wasn't just earth down there.

It was light.

Heat.

Color.

A spiraling funnel of gold and crimson, howling with ancestral voices. Some cried. Some laughed. Some whispered names that hadn't been spoken in generations.

Rayne's name was one of them.

She gripped the edge of the altar as a wind rose from the pit—hot, dry, violent. It carried salt and memory and bone. Her skin stung. Her eyes burned.

And then, the voices began to speak as one:

"The covenant has been broken. The land requires balance. Blood must answer blood."

Rayne tried to stand, but the pull was too strong. Her feet slid. Her arms burned. Chase grabbed her, teeth clenched, dragging her up the slope, cursing between gasps.

Callie didn't move.

Rayne looked back and saw her cousin kneeling, face lifted toward the sky, arms wide.

"No!" Rayne shouted. "Callie!"

But Callie didn't hear her—or chose not to.

Her lips moved in chant.

Her eyes glowed faint white.

"I remember now," she whispered. "I remember the vow. I remember the salt. I remember what she did."

"Callie!" Rayne lunged forward again, but Chase held her back.

"She's gone, Rayne. We'll all be gone if we don't move."

"We can't leave her..."

"She's not leaving this place. And neither are we if you don't run."

Behind them, the pit groaned louder.

Something was coming up through it.

Not a creature.

Not a spirit.

A presence.

The kind that made the trees hold their breath.

Rayne felt it in her teeth.

In her spine.

She turned.

And ran.

ΔΔΔ

They didn't stop until the sky turned black.

No stars.

No moon.

Only the red light still pulsing behind them like a heartbeat they could no longer ignore.

Rayne collapsed at the edge of a stream, her body shaking. Chase dropped beside her, panting, bleeding from his palms and knees.

They said nothing for a long time.

Just listened to the water.

The first true sound in hours.

"Callie..." Rayne whispered.

"She chose," Chase said, voice hollow. "The land chose her."

"No. It took her."

"No," he said again, this time firmer. "You saw her. She wanted it. She remembered something. She became something."

Rayne stared at the water. "I think we're next."

Chase didn't answer.

She dipped her fingers into the stream.

Warm.

Too warm.

Red.

Not muddy—thick red.

She yanked her hand back.

Blood.

The stream was running with blood.

And carved into the stones along the bank were symbols—the same spiral that had formed on the altar.

On her palm.

Rayne looked down.

The mark was still there.

Glowing softly.

"What does it mean?" she whispered.

Chase stood. His eyes were glassy.

"It means we're not escaping this. It's not just about the altar. Or the west. It's us. The whole line. Everything they tried to bury—it's awake now."

He turned, staring back toward the horizon.

"We're not walking through land anymore," he said. "We're walking through memory."

ΔΔΔ

They made shelter in a hollow tree that night, stuffing the entrance with moss and prayer. Rayne didn't sleep.

Every time she blinked, she saw Callie's face—glowing, reaching, then gone.

At dawn, she awoke to silence again.

But a figure stood in the clearing.

A woman, tall, dark-skinned, wrapped in layers of linen, her hair woven with shells. She looked like someone pulled from a time before fire.

Rayne stepped out slowly.

The woman didn't speak.

She pointed to Rayne's palm, then to the blood-red stream, then to the sky—where black birds circled.

Then she said only one word.

"Altar."

Rayne nodded, tears in her eyes.

"I know," she whispered. "We have to finish what they started."

The woman vanished.

ΔΔΔ

Later that day, they came to a flat plain dotted with ruins—a village that looked too familiar, yet out of time. Walls still stood, but they leaned. Trees grew through roofs.

At the center, a tower of stones piled in a spiral—reaching upward like a beckoning finger.

It pulsed.

Just once.

And then a voice rang out from nowhere—loud enough to shake the leaves from trees:

“Let the covenant sleep no longer.”

Rayne turned to Chase.

He didn’t move.

“Chase?”

His eyes had turned white.

Blood ran from his ears.

Rayne stepped back.

And the land below her cracked.

CHAPTER 4: THE COVENANT CRACKS

By dawn, the name Rayne had been carved into every doorframe in Rayden's Ridge. No one confessed to doing it. But every villager saw it. And no one dared erase it.

They gathered at the old crossroad—where four beaten paths met beneath the banyan tree—the place where old justice was once carried out.

They stood in silence.

No one argued. No one shouted. Even the goats dared not disrespect the atmosphere with sound.

Toria stepped forward, trembling—a descendant of the elder Victoria who once stood beside Grace, her name carried through a Ridge that had long tried to forget.

"We must call back what's been released. There is still time."

Christian shook his head.

"There is no calling back a god once it has opened its mouth."

"It is not a god," Angelique whispered. "God don't live in a box.

This... this is a covenant."

Alwin stared out toward the west. "It's a wound."

Laura held the dagger in both hands. It pulsed now. Softly. Like a heartbeat. She didn't know if it was hers.

ΔΔΔ

Children began drawing symbols in their sleep.

One boy, Chance, was found standing in the river, muttering the names of his ancestors in perfect order—names no one had taught him.

Another, Callie's younger brother, woke screaming, "It's in her bones! It's walking in her bones!"

When they asked him what "it" was, he said only, "The one she remembered."

Then he slept.

ΔΔΔ

Crops turned to salt.

Fruit hardened like stone.

And the land began to hum.

Not a song. Not a warning.

A rhythm.

Low. Constant. Ancient.

It came from below.

It shook spoons on shelves. It cracked mirrors. It twisted vines into the shape of spirals.

And at the edge of Rayden's Ridge, the pigs began walking into the river one by one, as if summoned.

No one stopped them.

ΔΔΔ

That night, Laura had a vision.

She stood inside a house made of bone. A woman stood with her back turned, humming something familiar. Her hair was long, braided with nettle and stone.

"Who are you?" Laura asked.

The woman turned.

Her face was Rayne's.

But her eyes were not.

They were deep—full of stars, ocean, and war.

"I am what comes after the covenant," she said.

Then she lifted her hand.

And the Ridge caught fire.

Laura woke screaming, sweat pouring from her skin.

Alwin held her, rocking her gently.

"She's—she's still out there… Rayne's still out there," she gasped.

"I left her… I left her out there—"

Her breath caught, breaking. "How did I forget her?"

Alwin held her tighter, his voice low, unsteady. "I forgot too."

A pause.

"We let her go."

He swallowed, like the words cost him something. "I don't know how... but we did."

The veil that had been cast over the village was slowly breaking.

ΔΔΔ

By the seventh day, the elders gave up.

Christian refused to speak. Toria had locked herself in the chapel and hadn't moved. The chickens lay dead in a perfect spiral around the water trough. Salt poured from the well. The youngest children refused to open their eyes, even while awake—crawling to feel the warmth of the pulse in the ground.

And the figure in flame-skin returned.

It walked down the main road at noon.

This time, no one ran.

It passed by the houses, touching each one. And where it touched, the wood blackened, the stone cracked, and the air turned thick.

When it reached the center of Rayden's Ridge, it raised both arms.

And from its mouth came a sound no human could survive.

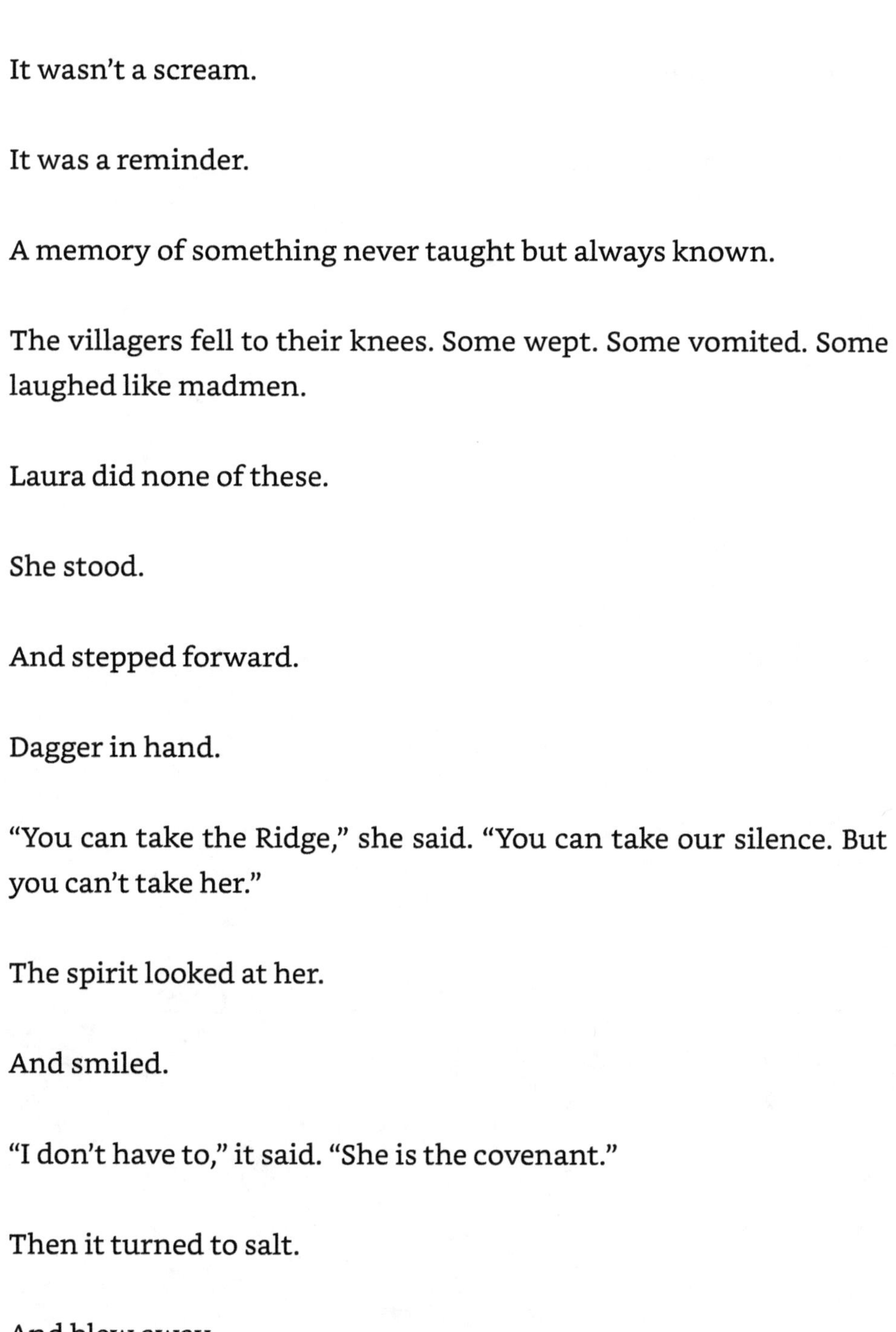

It wasn't a scream.

It was a reminder.

A memory of something never taught but always known.

The villagers fell to their knees. Some wept. Some vomited. Some laughed like madmen.

Laura did none of these.

She stood.

And stepped forward.

Dagger in hand.

"You can take the Ridge," she said. "You can take our silence. But you can't take her."

The spirit looked at her.

And smiled.

"I don't have to," it said. "She is the covenant."

Then it turned to salt.

And blew away.

Leaving only silence.

Then the west answered in thunder.

CHAPTER 5: WHEN THE FIRE FELL

The air had weight now.

Rayne could feel it pressing against her ribs, hanging from her lashes, crawling under her fingernails. It wasn't just heat. It was memory. The kind that lives in the bones of trees, the marrow of stones, and the flow of water.

They hadn't spoken since Chase's eyes turned white.

He walked in front now—silent, distant, following the pull like a bloodhound. His feet moved without pause—even when they bled. Rayne followed close behind, afraid to call his name, afraid he might answer... or worse, not.

They crossed through fields of ash that had never burned, passed rivers that ran backward, and over roots that throbbed like arteries. The land was alive. Not metaphorically. Truly alive—awakened and watching.

The covenant was no longer sleeping.

It was breathing.

And hungry.

ΔΔΔ

On the third day, they reached the bone wall.

It stretched from cliff to cliff—a lattice of femurs, spines, and shattered skulls. The center held a gate made of ribs tied together with tendons. At its base was a bowl filled with fire—not flames, but burning water, blue and gold.

Chase stopped walking.

He turned slowly, eyes no longer white—just empty. His voice was dry smoke.

"One must bleed."

Rayne stepped forward. "Chase?"

He pointed at the gate. "One must offer memory. Blood is not enough."

"I don't understand."

He took the dagger from his belt—the one they had found near Callie's body, after the altar cracked. He pressed the blade to his palm, but Rayne grabbed his wrist.

"No. Not like this."

“The gate won’t open unless we pay,” he said.

Rayne looked at her hands. The spiral on her palm had begun to spread—crawling toward her wrist, glowing faintly like fire under skin.

“I’ll do it,” she said.

Chase didn’t argue.

She stepped forward, knelt at the bowl, and squeezed the edge of the spiral until blood spilled into the flames.

At first, nothing happened.

Then the wall sighed—a low, guttural exhale. The bones creaked. The hair cords snapped.

And the gate opened.

Beyond it lay a corridor of mirrors, and behind each mirror—a piece of their past.

Rayne saw herself at age five, standing in her mother’s garden, listening to a song only she could hear.

Chase saw himself burying a bird, whispering the names of his ancestors before he even knew what ancestors were.

The mirrors whispered:

"This is what you gave. This is what you must leave behind."

Rayne touched the glass.

It shattered.

And the fire fell.

ΔΔΔ

The fire did not fall like rain.

It fell like the ending of a life.

It poured from the sky in sheets of color and pain—violet, black, deep red. It did not burn skin, but the soul. It touched their thoughts. Lit their forgotten traumas. Sparked their secret fears.

Rayne screamed.

Not from heat—from remembering.

She remembered everything. Helen's voice. Grace's silence. The night Laura buried the blade in the earth and said, "We will not speak of this again."

But the earth remembered.

The fire wasn't sent to destroy.

It was sent to reveal.

ΔΔΔ

Rayne stumbled through the mirror corridor as the flames licked the air around her. Glass shattered at her feet, but her skin did not bleed. Instead, her feet glowed—veins alight, pulsing with the same rhythm as the altar.

Chase followed, eyes wide. The fire danced over him but did not burn.

Behind them, voices rose.

"You are not the first."

"You are not the last."

"The covenant is not punishment. It is promise."

Rayne fell to her knees before a tall obsidian door, carved with the faces of women—dozens of them, all looking inward. The spiral in her hand pulsed once, then stopped.

Chase caught up, voice shaking. “This is it. The center.”

Rayne stood, hand trembling as she reached for the door.

It opened on its own.

Inside was silence.

And then—song.

Low and rhythmic, like humming through stone.

Rayne looked around and realized the room itself was stone. Names had been carved into it—names that glowed softly as they passed.

Helen. Grace. Others long forgotten.

In the center sat a pedestal of salt.

And on it, a single object:

The Covenant Scroll—made not of paper, but skin.

Rayne stepped forward.

As she approached, her palm burned again.

“Wait,” Chase said. “If you touch it, you seal it.”

"I already did," Rayne whispered. "When I read the journal. When I stepped onto the altar. When I chose not to forget."

She reached out and touched the scroll.

The fire stilled.

The land stopped shaking.

The air grew thick, then vanished into perfect silence.

Then the scroll opened itself.

And screamed.

ΔΔΔ

Rayne staggered back as wind and ash erupted from the scroll, spiraling upward in a cyclone of voice and light.

Images flashed—visions not of the past, but of the first covenant. A group of women standing on a cliff. Offering blood. Offering silence. Binding something not evil, but ancient. Wild.

And then breaking that promise—for love. For family. For power.

Rayne saw Helen's face as she walked away from the blood circle.

She saw Grace trying to fix it.

And she saw herself, standing at the edge of a new cliff, holding the scroll, holding the blade, holding the last word.

A choice burned inside her.

"Choose," the voices whispered. "Bind us again, or let the fire finish what it started."

Chase stepped beside her.

"What happens if you bind it?"

Rayne stared into the cyclone.

"We forget again."

"And if we don't?"

Rayne looked down at the burning world through the open door. Trees falling. Rivers drying. Salt pouring from the sky.

She looked at her hand.

"I don't know."

ΔΔΔ

She turned to the pedestal. Raised the scroll.

And screamed her own name into the fire.

The flames stopped.

Everything went still.

Then...

Callie's voice echoed through the chamber:

"You are not done."

The scroll dissolved into salt.

The pedestal cracked.

The floor gave way.

Rayne and Chase fell—into darkness.

Into heat.

Into the center of the covenant.

CHAPTER 6: THE SLAUGHTER GROUND

They landed in silence.

No thud. No pain. No resistance.

Just a slow, wet sound—like falling into blood.

Rayne's breath seized as her feet sank ankle-deep into soft, pulsing ground. The floor below her moved with the rhythm of a heart. It was not dirt. It was not stone.

It was flesh.

She looked around. Everything pulsed—the walls, the sky, the trees that weren't trees. Tendrils of red light arched over them like veins through skin. The air smelled of iron and birth and grief.

It reminded her of an old saying—of giants that once climbed the mountains, only to fall and become them, their blood and muscle hardening into the forbidden salt they called Himma. And here she was now, feeling those words with every step.

This wasn't a place. It was a body.

They were inside the covenant.

Chase was beside her, silent, eyes glassy. Blood leaked from his nose, but he didn't seem to notice. His lips moved as if praying, but no sound came out.

Rayne felt the spiral on her hand begin to twist.

It didn't glow anymore.

It ached.

Something was coming.

Not fast. Not loud.

But final.

ΔΔΔ

At Rayden's Ridge, the soil split.

Not cracked—split. Like lips parting to speak a truth that was withheld too long.

Out of the gap came hands.

Not human hands.

They were long. Dry. Gray. Wrapped in cloth soaked through with salt. Each finger carried a name. Some names still lived in the Ridge. Some had died long ago.

Christian ran to the church bell.

He rang it once.

The rope broke in his hand.

The ground howled.

Then the people began to bleed.

Not from wounds. From memory.

Noses. Ears. Eyes.

Every remembered name—spoken or hidden—began to pull itself free from their mouths.

Children wept the names of ancestors they'd never learned.

Mothers screamed the names of babies lost in wombs.

And Laura stood in the center of it all, dagger raised, staring west.

"It's begun," she whispered.

ΔΔΔ

Inside the covenant, Rayne walked forward.

Each step squelched.

She could feel things beneath the skin of the ground—moving, waiting.

The path led her to a mound.

And on the mound stood a woman.

She wore a dress of red leaves, her skin ash-gray, her face masked in gold.

“Who are you?” Rayne whispered.

The woman didn’t answer.

She raised her hand.

And Rayne’s body convulsed.

Every memory—of Helen, of Grace, of Callie, of herself — poured out through her mouth in a wail that shook the ground.

The woman spoke at last:

“You are the slaughter. You are the seed. You are what they tried to bury.”

Chase dropped to his knees beside her.

He began to vomit salt.

His skin blistered.

The ground beneath him opened.

Rayne tried to crawl toward him, but her arms wouldn't work.

The woman in red leaves descended the mound and knelt beside her.

She whispered in Rayne's ear:

"You will not leave here with all of you."

Then the sky split.

And the slaughter began.

ΔΔΔ

The sky tore open with a scream.

A sound older than language—layered with sobs, chants, moans. Not voices from above, but beneath. From under every root Rayne had stepped on. From under every stone laid at the Ridge. The wail of the earth remembering what was done to it.

And what it was owed.

Flames poured downward, not upward.

But not like fire.

Like old wounds learning how to burn again.

Rayne watched as the woman in red leaves stood, arms wide, welcoming the fire. It touched her and turned her into wind. A wind of names.

They swept past Rayne and Chase—into their mouths, their ears, their scars.

Chase screamed as the salt left his veins.

He collapsed, twitching.

Rayne tried to speak but her jaw had locked. She heard whispers coming from her own skin.

One voice louder than the rest.

It was Callie.

"You brought us here. You woke what they buried."

Rayne sobbed. “I didn’t mean to.”

"Meaning is for the living." Callie replied.

Rayne gasped—then her chest opened, not torn, not broken, but unfurled from within. A light spilled from her sternum, bright as a second sun, burning through the slaughter.

It revealed the truth of the ground they stood on:

It was a field of bones.

Thousands.

Some old. Some fresh.

Some… still breathing.

Chase sat up suddenly. His eyes were not his.

They were Helen’s.

He looked at Rayne and said:

“She is watching. She is weeping.”

Then he stood and walked toward the bones.

And knelt.

The bones moved, wrapping around him like a throne.

Rayne screamed. “Chase!”

But he only whispered, “This is how it ends.”

ΔΔΔ

At Rayden’s Ridge, the people fell one by one.

Some dropped silently, eyes open to nothing.

Others screamed names until their throats gave out.

Some were pulled into the trees—the branches alive, lashing, dragging.

Laura stood alone.

She had made her choice.

She raised the dagger—then lowered it, like the choice had already been made for her.

She turned and headed west.

ΔΔΔ

In the slaughterfield, Rayne crawled.

The bones cut her hands, her knees. But she didn't stop.

She had no plan. Only instinct.

She crawled toward the heart.

She didn't know what it looked like—but she felt it.

It beat just ahead, under the soft flesh of this world.

A mound, pulsing. Covered in salt and ash.

She pressed her hand to it.

The spiral on her palm flared, then vanished.

She whispered:

"I offer my memory. I offer my name. I offer my end."

The mound opened.

Light filled her.

Pain tore her.

She saw everything—the beginning of the covenant, the faces of the first women, the moment the first silence was agreed upon.

And she saw the lie.

The covenant had never been about peace.

It was about delay.

Blood must answer blood.

Always.

Rayne began to burn from the inside out.

But she didn't scream.

She sang.

A song made of all the names.

A song made of wind and fire and promise.

And the slaughter slowed.

ΔΔΔ

Chase rose from the throne of bones.

His face was wet.

His eyes were his own.

He walked to Rayne, now glowing like a dying sun, and knelt.

"Rayne."

She looked at him—but the glow in her eyes was gone.

Only light remained.

She reached up.

Touched his chest.

And whispered, "Finish it."

Then she collapsed.

A wave of silence exploded from her body.

It rolled across the slaughterfield.

Across the Ridge.

Across every name that had ever been spoken.

And time… held its breath.

ΔΔΔ

At the broken altar back west, a single flower bloomed.

At Rayden’s Ridge, Laura fell to her knees.

"I'm too late."

The salt stopped falling.

The children opened their eyes.

And in the burning center of the covenant, Chase stood alone.

Holding the last memory of Rayne.

And listening.

Because now…

the land was quiet again.

But he knew silence never lasted long.

CHAPTER 7: GRACE'S STAND

She woke in salt.

Not water. Not earth. Only salt.

It clung to her skin like ash, coated her tongue, stung her eyes. She couldn't breathe at first—not because of pain, but because the silence was too long. It wasn't the stillness of death. It was the stillness of judgment.

Grace Fana rose slowly from the cracked altar where she had once sat.

She had been in the in-between for too long. A spirit not yet gone, a woman barely remembered. She was the guardian of the covenant—a whisper in its spine. But now she felt it.

The silence had broken.

The child had awakened the core.

And the slaughter had begun.

"Rayne..." she whispered.

But the girl didn't answer.

Grace stood.

The salt broke beneath her feet like brittle memory.

The altar glowed faintly.

And the west called once more.

ΔΔΔ

The land remembered Grace.

As she walked, the trees leaned back in recognition.

The wind rose to kiss her cheeks.

Even the crows—usually silent—cawed three times and flew east. As if to carry her name.

She passed through the same broken field where Helen had once stood with fire in her hands and fear in her womb. Grace paused there. Bent down. Pressed her fingers into the earth.

“Let me in,” she whispered.

The ground opened, just a crack.

She stepped through.

ΔΔΔ

Chase saw her first.

He was kneeling in the heart of the covenant, holding what remained of Rayne—not body, not ash, but light.

He heard footsteps.

Turned.

And saw Grace.

Alive.

Whole.

Walking through the field of bones like she had grown there.

He tried to stand, but couldn't.

"You," he gasped. "You were supposed to stop this."

"I tried," Grace said, kneeling beside him. "But my sacrifice wasn't enough. The covenant was already rotting. It needed something purer."

"Rayne..."

"She gave more than herself. She gave remembrance. And now the land knows."

Chase looked down at his hands.

"They're not done, are they?"

Grace shook her head.

"No. But I am."

She kissed his forehead.

And whispered a final word into the bones.

The spiral flared once more—brighter than ever.

Then dissolved into ash.

And the bones beneath Chase shifted—not to trap him, but to lift him. Like a cradle.

Grace stood tall, arms open, her back to the collapsing ridge of bones behind her. The entire slaughter ground was still. Watching.

Grace rose slowly. Her gaze turned east.

"Not yet," she whispered.

And the wind took her.

ΔΔΔ

Rayden's Ridge was dying.

The people had stopped screaming.

Not because peace had come.

Because there were no more words.

Names had been spent like currency, and still the covenant was unsatisfied.

Salt poured from the sky again—slower now, but heavier.

Children held their mouths open and swallowed it like communion.

In the church, Toria sat catatonic.

Angelique lit herbs no one remembered the names of.

And Laura?

Laura had vanished.

Some said she walked west.

Others said she walked into the fire.

Only one soul walked against the wind that day.

Grace.

She stepped into the Ridge barefoot, her eyes glowing like moonlight caught in water.

And every elder dropped to their knees.

“You,” whispered Christian, his voice cracking.

“You’re dead.”

Grace smiled softly.

“No,” she said. “I was forgotten. There’s a difference.”

Then she spoke to the wind and fire,

"Protect what the covenant had not yet taken."

And then the wind carried her west.

ΔΔΔ

As if waiting for her return the land itself whispered:

“One more.”

Chase flinched.

Grace stepped from the wind behind him.

She stepped onto the mound where Rayne had bled out her name. The light was still warm there. Still humming.

She raised both hands to the sky.

And called out:

“I am Grace Fana. Daughter of Helen. Keeper of silence. Breaker of vow. I come not to bind, but to end.”

The clouds rolled.

The flesh-sky above them peeled like fruit.

From the open sky descended the covenant made flesh—not a god, not a demon. A being made of every unspoken name, every severed tongue, every forgotten grave.

It had a hundred eyes.

It had no mouth.

It moved like sorrow.

Grace faced it without flinching.

"You are pain," she said. "But I was born in you."

The being lowered itself.

Bowed.

But did not speak.

Because it could not.

It was silence made manifest.

And silence could not grant mercy.

It could only wait.

Grace reached into her chest.

Her own spiral burned now—not on her skin, but deep within.

She pulled it out with a cry.

Held it in her hand like a coal.

"This is my offering."

She dropped it.

The mound opened again.

The light this time was black.

And the Ridge screamed.

ΔΔΔ

Far away, Laura collapsed in the dirt.

Her vision went white.

She saw Helen holding a baby.

She saw Grace screaming in the wind.

She saw Rayne walking backward into the sea.

And she saw herself.

Holding the blade.

At the edge of the Ridge.

"Choose," a voice said.

But she didn't know who it belonged to anymore.

ΔΔΔ

At the center of the slaughterground, Grace began to sing.

A song with no melody.

Only name after name after name.

Each name a flame.

Each flame a funeral.

The being trembled.

Its eyes closed.

And one by one, they began to fall from its body.

Eyes became seeds.

Seeds became blood.

Blood became flowers.

Red ones.

Bright.

Soft.

Growing through the bones.

Growing through the salt.

Growing through the silence.

Then Rayne's voice moved through the wind:

"We are not done."

ΔΔΔ

Chase reached out, stunned, eyes filled with tears.

"Grace… Rayne... Callie..."

Callie did not follow. She had never left.

But Grace had already fallen.

Rayne was gone with her.

Grace's body faded into petals.

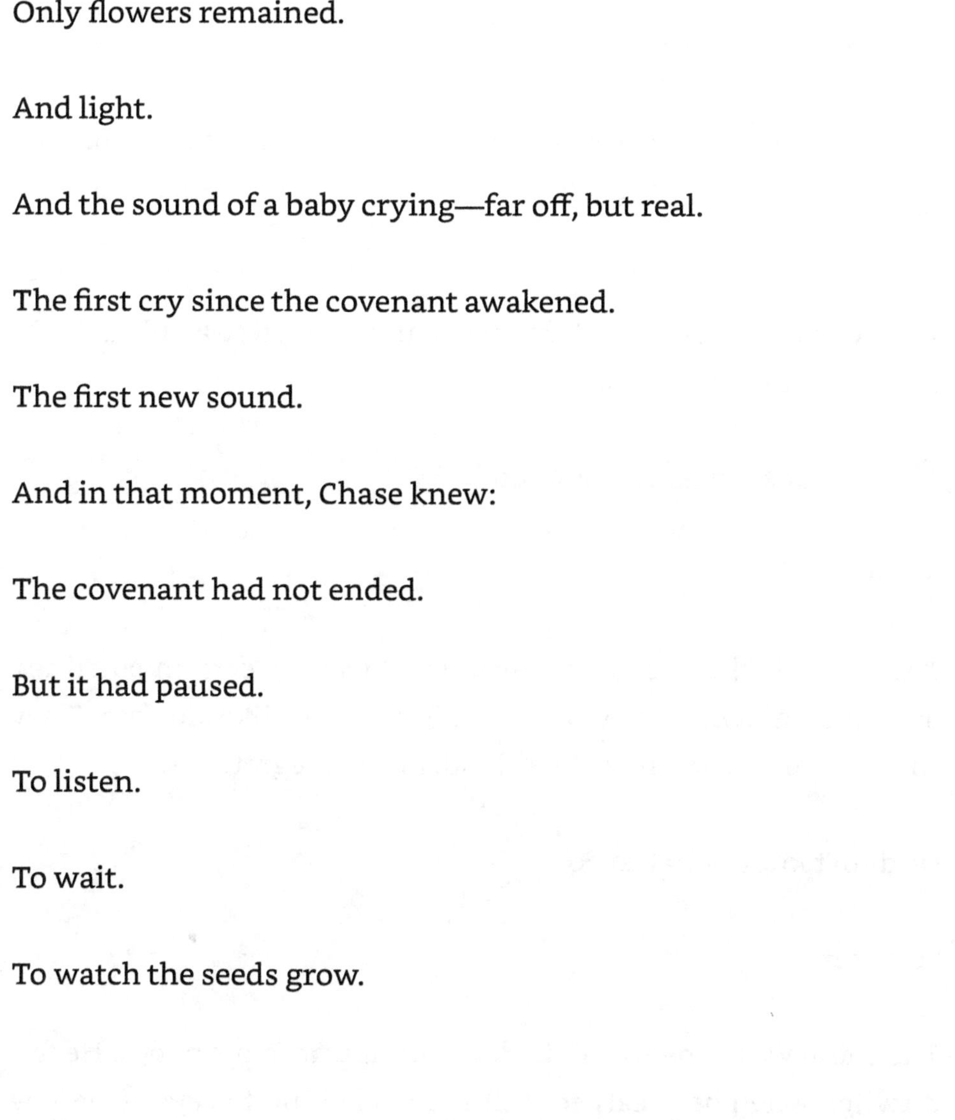

And then wind.

And then nothing.

Only flowers remained.

And light.

And the sound of a baby crying—far off, but real.

The first cry since the covenant awakened.

The first new sound.

And in that moment, Chase knew:

The covenant had not ended.

But it had paused.

To listen.

To wait.

To watch the seeds grow.

CHAPTER 8: THE SILENCE AFTER

The earth was still.

For the first time in weeks—maybe months, maybe centuries—who knows—it did not groan, scream, bleed, or pulse. It simply... held.

The sky, once swollen with fire and names, faded to a dull gray. No birds. No rain. Just silence.

And in that silence, Chase stood.

Alone.

The mound where Grace had vanished was covered in small red blossoms, glowing faintly. They didn't smell like flowers. They smelled like warm bread, like blood, like old regret.

He didn't know what to do.

So he sat.

The spiral was gone from his skin, but not from his bones. He felt it twitch when he breathed. Felt it burn behind his eyes when he closed them. He was no longer just a boy who followed two girls into a myth.

He was the myth now.

Or what was left of it.

ΔΔΔ

Rayden's Ridge hadn't fully healed.

But the screaming had stopped.

The salt no longer poured.

Children began speaking in their own voices again. The elders walked like shadows, barely touching the earth. Toria emerged from the chapel, her hair streaked white, her eyes milk-glass clear. She said nothing.

Just lit a fire.

And burned every book in the library.

Laura returned too.

No one saw her arrive.

That day, she was simply there again—standing beside the flowered altar with a black cloth around her hand. She said

Rayne's name once, then planted a seed beside the largest blossom.

She didn't explain what the seed was.

She just said, "She told me to."

And that was enough.

ΔΔΔ

Back at the edge of the slaughterground, Chase wandered. The bones no longer shifted. The ground no longer moved. But he didn't trust it.

He walked in spirals.

Following instinct.

Following memory.

One night, he found the journal.

Rayne's journal.

Dry. Preserved. Resting on a stone like someone had placed it there for him.

He opened it.

Inside were only two words, scrawled in blood:

“Not done.”

His hands shook.

Then from far off, he heard it.

A drumbeat.

Not war.

Not warning.

A heartbeat.

And then—footsteps.

Slow.

Certain.

And a child’s voice:

“Are you him?”

Chase turned.

Saw a girl.

No older than seven.

Hair in twists.

Eyes bright.

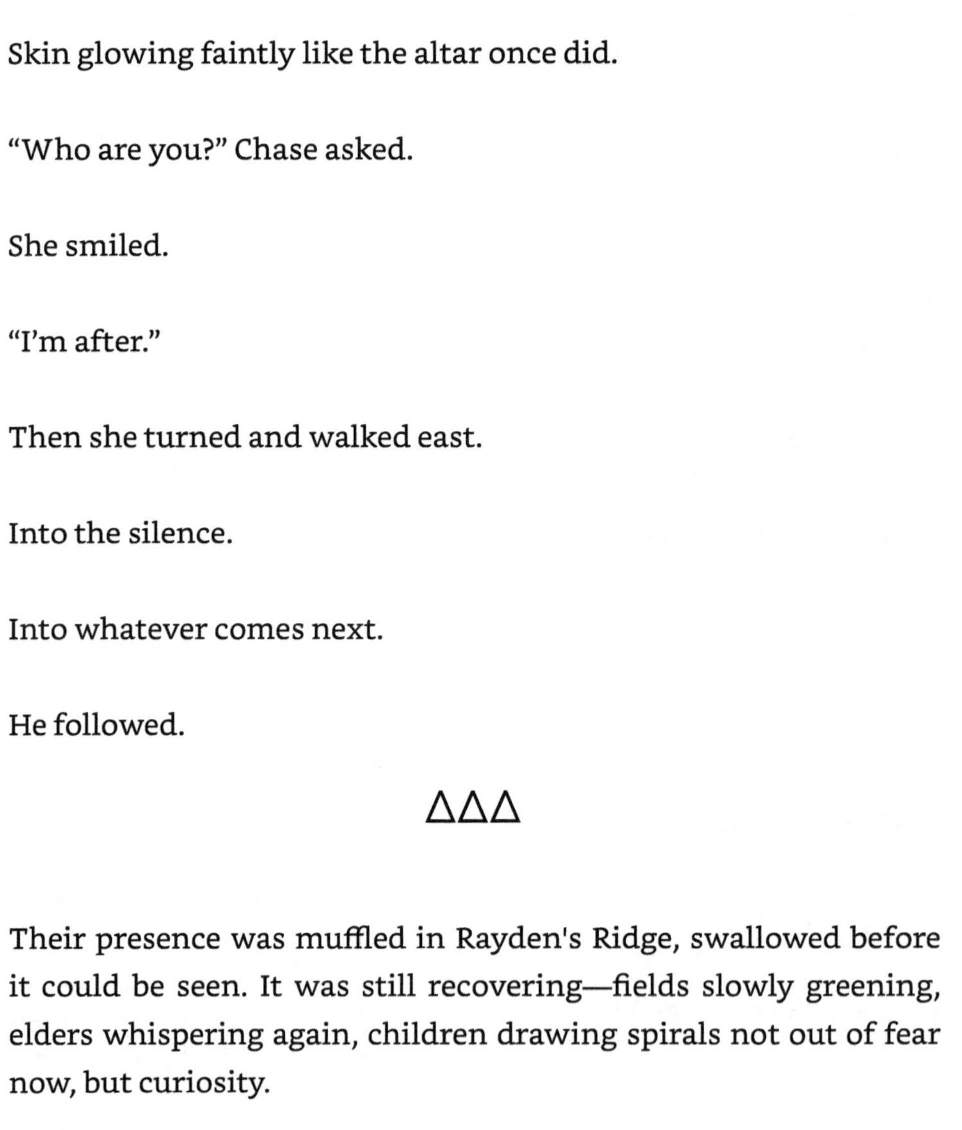

Skin glowing faintly like the altar once did.

"Who are you?" Chase asked.

She smiled.

"I'm after."

Then she turned and walked east.

Into the silence.

Into whatever comes next.

He followed.

ΔΔΔ

Their presence was muffled in Rayden's Ridge, swallowed before it could be seen. It was still recovering—fields slowly greening, elders whispering again, children drawing spirals not out of fear now, but curiosity.

They crossed the river, shallow with a handful of fish again. Its waters were red-tinted, but calm. Chase looked at his reflection once.

It didn't blink.

His face was harder now. Not older. Just worn.

He looked behind them.

The Ridge seemed smaller somehow. Or maybe he'd just gotten larger.

Ahead, the child hummed.

Each note made a bird land nearby.

Each step left small imprints in the ground.

They reached the old chapel ruins on the outskirts of the Ridge—a place once full of sacred stories and forgotten rules.

Inside, the fire still burned.

But it burned upward.

Into the sky.

And floating above the flame was something new:

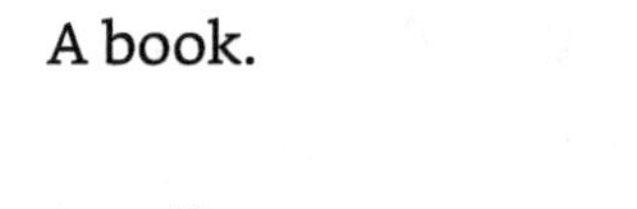

A book.

Small.

Bound in black and braided hair.

Chase stepped forward.

The child nodded.

"This is what comes next," she said.

He opened it.

Only one sentence waited inside:

"Tell the truth, or repeat the silence."

ΔΔΔ

Back at the town center of Rayden's Ridge, flowers grew where bodies had once vanished.

And someone had scratched a message into the stone wall where Grace first stood when she returned:

"If you forget again, you deserve what comes next."

Laura saw it.

She didn't erase it.

Instead, she planted herbs beside it.

ΔΔΔ

Chase did not sleep that night.

He read the book again and again, though it never changed.

Tell the truth, or repeat the silence.

He closed it, then stood, then faced the child.

"What's your name?" he asked.

She smiled.

"I don't have one yet."

He blinked.

"Then what should I call you?"

She pointed at the burning sky behind them.

"Call me Lucy."

Then she walked into the trees.

And disappeared.

ΔΔΔ

Chase turned to the fire.

Sat beside it.

Opened the journal Rayne left him.

And wrote the first sentence of the new covenant:

"Once, we broke the silence, and the silence broke us back..."

He didn't stop writing until morning.

Not because the story was done.

But because the land had started listening again.

ΔΔΔ

Morning came quiet.

No birds.

No wind.

Just light.

Soft, golden, clean—like the world was trying to forgive itself.

Chase sat at the edge of the Ridge, feet dangling over the same cliff where Helen once stood with fire in her hand. Below him, red blossoms had taken over the ground—not in rows, not in random patterns, but in spirals.

The covenant wasn't undone.

It had simply changed shape.

He turned to the last page of Rayne's journal.

Blank.

He dipped his fingers in ash from the fire and wrote three more words:

"We remember now."

Then he tore the page out, folded it carefully, and slid it under a stone at the altar's base.

If anyone ever came looking, they'd find it.

And they'd know this wasn't myth.

It was memory.

It was blood.

It was warning.

Chase stood.

He wasn't sure who he was now—a witness, a brother, a seed.

But he knew one thing.

It wasn't over.

And as he stepped back into the Ridge...

A newborn cried somewhere behind him.

And the wind whispered again.

"We are not done, Chase."

CHAPTER 9: OUROBOROS

The wind came first.

It moved like it had somewhere to be—not the lazy breeze of memory, but the sharp wind of consequence. It swept across Rayden's Ridge, lifting ash, stirring petals, waking the roots of things buried too deep.

It carried names.

Chase heard them.

Whispered in the rustle of trees. Spoken from cracks in walls. Hissed from the mouths of those who hadn't spoken in days.

Grace. Helen. Rayne. Laura. Callie. Lucy.

But his own name?

Unspoken.

Not because it had been forgotten.

Because it hadn't been claimed.

Not yet.

He stood at the altar for the last time.

The journal was open. The flame still danced in the chapel hearth. The flower where Grace fell had bloomed again, but this time the petals were black tipped with red.

The land wasn't mourning.

It was marking.

A shadow moved behind him.

He turned.

It was Laura.

Older. Thinner. Tired in ways no sleep could fix.

"Heard you wrote it all down," she said.

"I tried."

"Try again."

She handed him a small piece of cloth—black, wrapped in bone thread.

Inside: a tooth.

Rayne's.

Chase stared.

"You kept this?"

"She left it," Laura said. "At the base of the spiral."

He didn't ask how.

He just nodded.

Folded the cloth again.

Tucked it into his pocket.

Then said, "I think she's coming back."

Laura didn't flinch.

"She never left."

ΔΔΔ

That night, the Ridge dreamed as one.

Children, elders, goats—even the trees shook in unison.

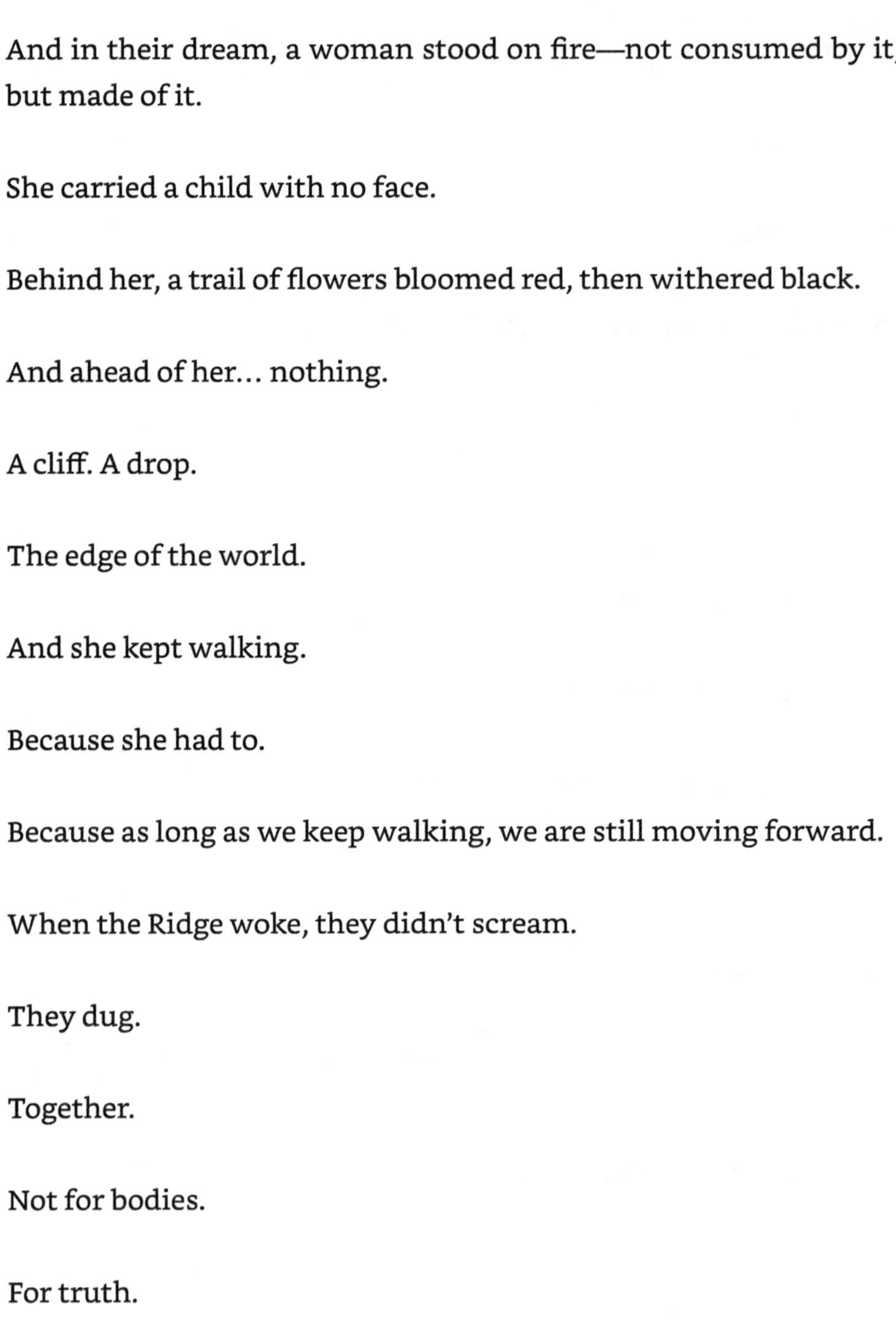

And in their dream, a woman stood on fire—not consumed by it, but made of it.

She carried a child with no face.

Behind her, a trail of flowers bloomed red, then withered black.

And ahead of her… nothing.

A cliff. A drop.

The edge of the world.

And she kept walking.

Because she had to.

Because as long as we keep walking, we are still moving forward.

When the Ridge woke, they didn't scream.

They dug.

Together.

Not for bodies.

For truth.

They uncovered bones beneath the prayer house.

Not of saints—but of those unremembered.

Women. Children. Men with their tongues turned to stone.

One skeleton was buried holding a bundle of braided hair.

The bundle hummed.

They left it there.

No one dared to touch it.

ΔΔΔ

Chase lit a fire at the altar.

Not for ritual.

For warmth.

Around it gathered twelve villagers—each from a line that had touched the covenant.

Each with a mark.

Each with a story.

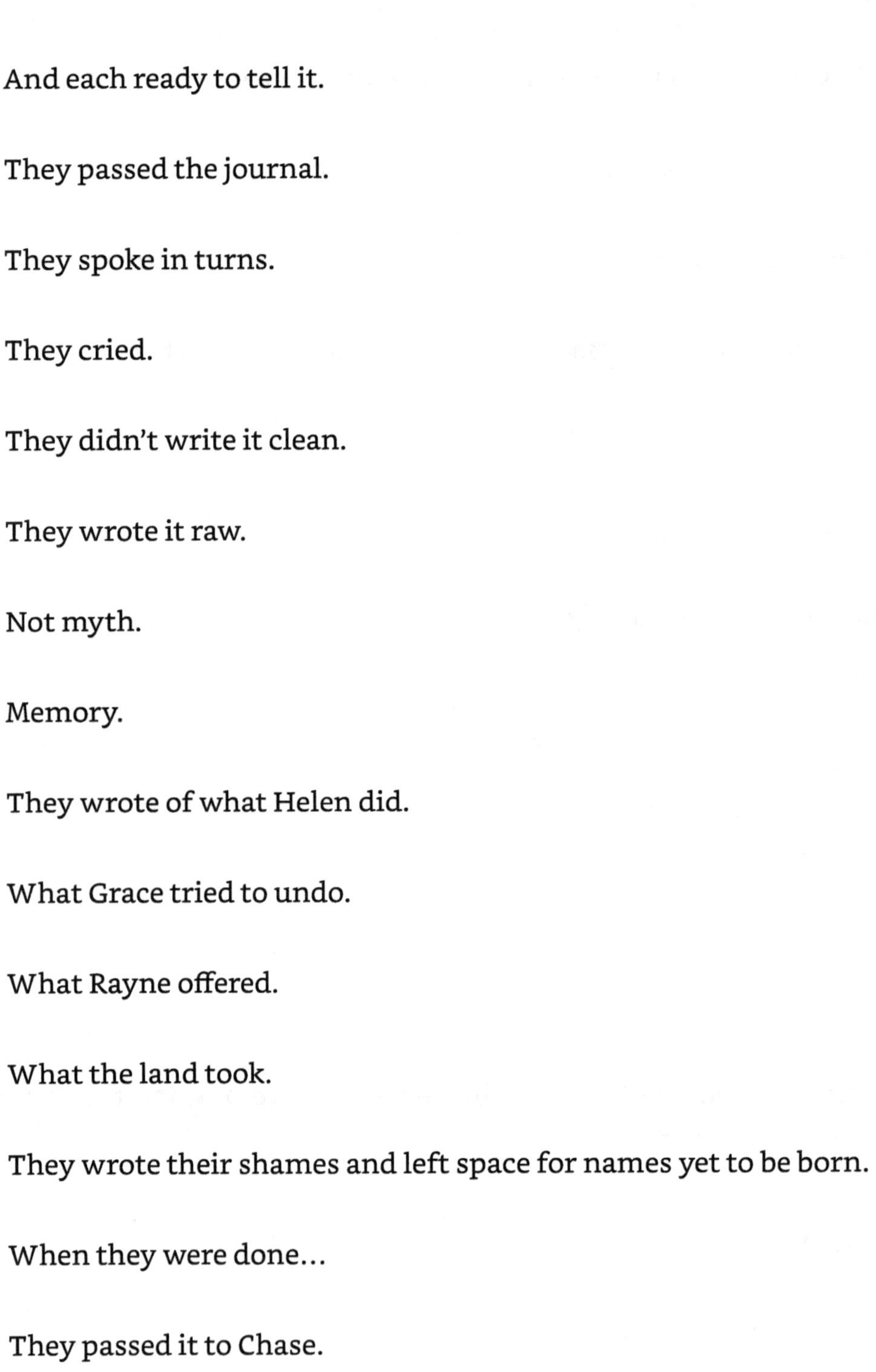

And each ready to tell it.

They passed the journal.

They spoke in turns.

They cried.

They didn't write it clean.

They wrote it raw.

Not myth.

Memory.

They wrote of what Helen did.

What Grace tried to undo.

What Rayne offered.

What the land took.

They wrote their shames and left space for names yet to be born.

When they were done...

They passed it to Chase.

And said, "Read."

And he did.

Even when his voice cracked.

Even when salt dripped from the pages.

He read until the sun reached the altar.

Until the Ridge listened.

And when he reached the last page—

Blank—

He wrote four more words:

"We are not done."

ΔΔΔ

Then a child stood.

Not Lucy.

But one born of the same light.

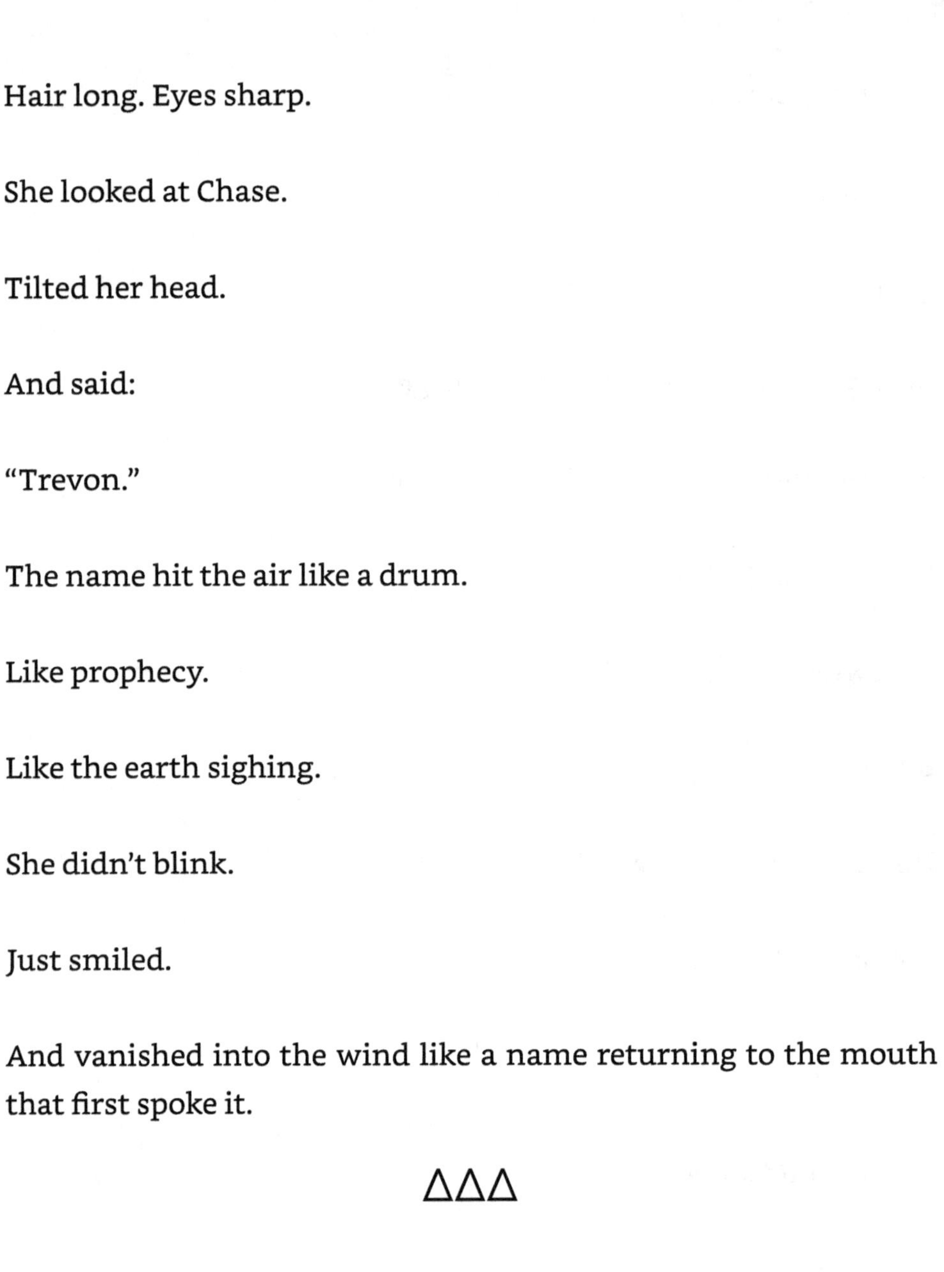

Hair long. Eyes sharp.

She looked at Chase.

Tilted her head.

And said:

"Trevon."

The name hit the air like a drum.

Like prophecy.

Like the earth sighing.

She didn't blink.

Just smiled.

And vanished into the wind like a name returning to the mouth that first spoke it.

ΔΔΔ

The Ridge stood in silence.

Then one by one, the villagers knelt.

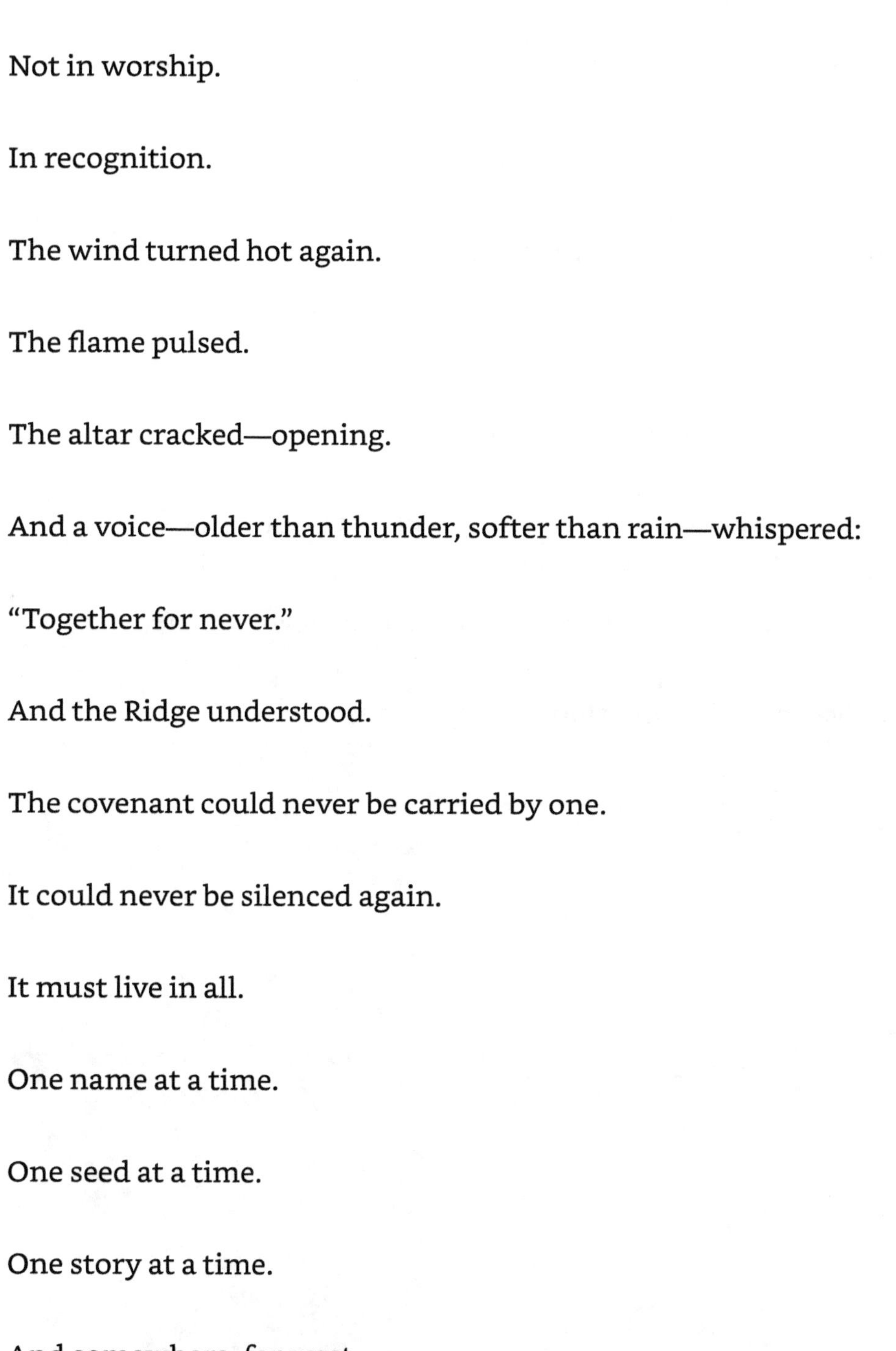

Not in worship.

In recognition.

The wind turned hot again.

The flame pulsed.

The altar cracked—opening.

And a voice—older than thunder, softer than rain—whispered:

“Together for never.”

And the Ridge understood.

The covenant could never be carried by one.

It could never be silenced again.

It must live in all.

One name at a time.

One seed at a time.

One story at a time.

And somewhere, far west...

A baby cried.

Then laughed.

Then said, for the very first time—

"We."

And the land bloomed—in spirals.

Because sometimes, saving the world and destroying it are the same act—and by the time you know which one you've done, the circle has already decided.

www.ingramcontent.com/pod-product-compliance
Lightning Source LLC
LaVergne TN
LVHW011047110826
845149LV00015B/3394

9781968581077